7/14

for Marcus

Published in 2013 by Simply Read Books www.simplyreadbooks.com
Text & Illustrations © 2013 Michael Moniz

Library and Archives Canada Cataloguing in Publication

Moniz, Michael
    The boy and the whale / written and illustrated by Michael Moniz.

ISBN 978-1-927018-14-9

    I. Title.

PS8626.O54B69 2013   jC813'.6   C2013-900933-7

We gratefully acknowledge for their financial support of our publishing program the Canada Council for the Arts, the BC Arts Council, and the Government of Canada through the Canada Book Fund (CBF).

Printed in Malaysia

Book design by Natasha Kanji and Michael Moniz

10 9 8 7 6 5 4 3 2 1

The Boy and the Whale

Michael Moniz

SIMPLY READ BOOKS

Long ago, on a tiny island floating in the middle of the big ocean ...

there lived a boy. His family was very poor and the boy had no brothers or sisters. He was lonely.

Every day, when the weather was nice, the boy would sail out to sea and cast his fishing line. He loved the ocean more than anything.

He would sit and daydream for hours, watching the waves, pausing only to reel in his catch.

His only company was the seagulls and other birds that circled his boat.

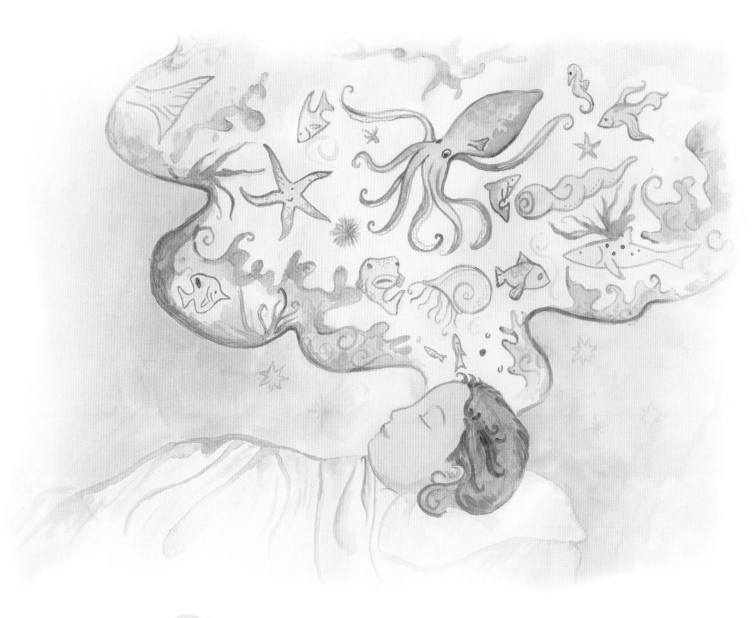

At night, the boy dreamed of the big ocean. All of its creatures, big and small, floated around in his head.

One day, while out at sea, the boy heard an eerie sound echoing in the distance. Curious, he sailed over to see what it was.

To the boy's surprise there was an enormous creature thrashing in the water — a whale. It was entangled in a huge net.

The young boy felt a swell of pity for the whale.

He grabbed pieces of the net, and with his small fishing knife, he cut and cut.

Suddenly, the whale broke free, crashing out of the water and jumping over the boy's boat.

The whale was gone, without a thank you or goodbye. The boy trembled in his rocking boat. He headed directly for shore.

The boy thought often of the whale in the weeks that followed.
One particularly stormy morning, he decided to fish from the safety of the
rocks, casting out as far as he could.

With a splash, a giant fish jumped out of the water with the boy's fishing lure hooked in its mouth. The boy was yanked off the rocks into the sea.

He didn't want to lose his fishing rod, so he held on tight and was dragged farther and farther by the fish.

Finally, the line snapped. The fishing pole jerked out of the boy's hands. He dove and grabbed it as quickly as he could.

The giant fish was gone. Land was only a speck in the distance.

He began to swim.

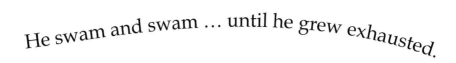

He swam and swam … until he grew exhausted.

"Help! Help!" he cried, but he was still too far away for anyone to hear.

All of a sudden, a huge flipper rose out from the waves.

Then an island grew beneath the boy, lifting him out of the water.

The island grew and grew, until at last the boy realized it was no island.

It was the whale.

The whale rumbled beneath him, waves lapping against its sides as it carried him towards land.

When they neared the coast, the boy climbed onto the rocks. The two looked at one another, the whale with curiosity and the boy with wonder. This was, without a doubt, the same creature the boy had rescued all those days ago.

The boy waved goodbye and watched the whale grow smaller and smaller as it swam towards the setting sun.

From then on, even though the little boy was poor he felt very lucky.

He knew he had a great friend in the whale.

As the boy grew into a man, he always remembered how far a little

kindness can go …

and how big a friend you can make along the way.

The End